First published in the United States in 2002 by North-South Books Inc.,
an imprint of NordSüd Verlag AG, Gossau Zürich, Switzerland.

Copyright © 2001 by NordSüd Verlag AG, Gossau Zürich, Switzerland
First published in Switzerland under the title *Kleiner Eisbär, hilf mir fliegen!*
English translation copyright © 2001 by North-South Books Inc.

First published in Great Britain, Canada, Australia, and New Zealand in 2001 by North-South Books Inc.,
an imprint of NordSüd Verlag AG, Gossau Zürich, Switzerland.
First paperback edition published in 2006 by North-South Books Inc. Distributed in
the United States by North-South Books Inc., New York.

Library of Congress Cataloging-in-Publication Data is available.
A CIP catalogue record for this book is available from The British Library.

ISBN-13: 978-0-7358-1533-9 / ISBN-10: 0-7358-1533-X (library edition)
1 3 5 7 9 LE 10 8 6 4 2

ISBN-13: 978-0-7358-2077-7 / ISBN-10: 0-7358-2077-5 (paperback edition)
1 3 5 7 9 PB 10 8 6 4 2

Printed in Belgium

Little Polar Bear
and the Big Balloon

Written and Illustrated by
Hans de Beer

Translated by Rosemary Lanning

NORTHSOUTH
BOOKS

New York / London

Lars, the Little Polar Bear, lived at the North Pole. He didn't mind the cold. He was used to ice and snow and chilly winds.

But today the sun was shining for a change, and Lars was basking in its warmth.

If I could have one wish, thought Lars, watching the seagulls circling high above him, I would like to fly. Perhaps not as high as they do, but . . .

A loud throbbing interrupted his daydream. It was a ship. That meant danger! Lars quickly slid off his ice floe.

Lars clung to the floe as it rocked on the waves. The ship came so close that it nearly brushed against him. When the ship had gone past, Lars started to climb back onto his ice floe.

Then a voice called: "Look out down there!" Something plummeted past him and disappeared underwater with a splash.

When Lars had recovered from his shock, he ducked under
the water to see what the "something" was. It was a strange
bird. Alarmed at the sight of a polar bear, the little bird tried
to swim away, but Lars swam underneath it and lifted it out
of the water.

"There's no need to be scared of me," he said. "I'm Lars,
the Little Polar Bear."

He spoke so kindly that the little bird stopped being
frightened at once.

"I'm Yuri, the little puffin," he said, smiling back at Lars.

"A puffin? I've never seen anyone like you before!" said the Little Polar Bear. "Where do you come from?"

"Far, far away from here," Yuri told him. "I was fishing one day, and I accidentally dipped my wings in an oil slick. I just managed to get onto that ship, but I couldn't lift my wings anymore. I've been on the ship for days and days with nothing to eat! Then I saw land at last, and here I am. Now I'll never get home again," he said sadly.

"Of course you will! I've helped lots of animals find their way home," Lars said comfortingly. "Look, the ship is dropping anchor. That's good."

"Why is it good?" asked Yuri.

"Because you'll need the ship to show you the way home."

"I can't help you fly," said Lars, "but I can make your
wings feel better. When we polar bears have a pain we always
go to the hot springs. I'll take you there. Follow me!"

The little puffin's webbed feet made it hard for him to keep
up with Lars.

"Flying really is the best way to travel," he sighed.

"I'm sure it is. I'd love to fly myself, but jump on my back
and we'll get there faster."

When at last they arrived at the steaming hot springs Lars
found it hard to persuade his little friend to get into the
bubbling water.

"Are you sure this won't hurt me?" Yuri asked anxiously.

But once he was in the water, Yuri enjoyed the warmth. Soon the oil had washed off his wings, but he still was too weak to fly. Disappointed, Lars and Yuri walked back to the ship.

They were almost back in the bay when they saw a huge ball ahead of them. Lars was shocked, but Yuri said calmly: "People fly in those things. I've seen them myself."

"Fly!" said Lars, laughing. "In something as big as that? With no wings?" He couldn't believe it.

Lars was curious. He wanted to examine the big, round thing more closely.

Yuri wasn't sure this was a good idea. "Come on, Lars," he said. "It's starting to snow."

But Lars was already climbing into the basket. He found cables and levers, buttons and little lights.

"Come here, Yuri! You've got to see this!" cried Lars eagerly, helping the little bird into the basket. As he did, he accidentally pushed something. There was a loud hiss. A flame shot up over their heads, and before Lars and Yuri knew what was happening, the balloon took off. It climbed higher and higher through the swirling snowflakes.

The basket was rocked and buffeted by the snowstorm. Lars and Yuri nervously huddled together, as far away as possible from the roaring flame above them.

When Yuri summoned up the courage to look over the edge of the basket, he saw they were already too high to jump out.

"We're flying higher and higher, Lars," said Yuri.

"Flying? Higher and higher?" Lars gulped.

"Yes, we're in the clouds," said Yuri.

"C-c-clouds?" stammered Lars, and he gulped again.

Suddenly the roaring stopped, the flame died down, and they floated peacefully above a sea of clouds.

"Look, Lars," cried Yuri excitedly. "See how wonderful it is to fly!"

Lars peered over the edge. The clouds were no longer above but below him now. Lars was amazed. But he was scared, too, because they were so high up.

"I think perhaps I can fly from this height!" Yuri declared, and before Lars could stop him the little puffin had launched himself into the air.

"See you later!" he cried as he disappeared into the clouds.

Lars was left on his own.

Lars held on tight as the balloon sank back into the clouds.

"Help, Yuri! Help!" cried Lars. But there was no answer.

Swaying violently, the balloon finally came out of the clouds, and Lars could see where he was going. And there was Yuri!

"Look, Lars! I can fly again!" he cried happily, and he was gone.

Lars was so pleased that he forgot his fear for a moment. Then he saw the ground getting closer and closer . . . !

But the Little Polar Bear was in luck. The basket slid gently over the snow-white ground. Before it came to a halt, Lars jumped out. Never had he felt so glad to be in deep, soft snow! Yuri flew up to him with a beak full of little fish.

"For you!" he said, laughing happily. "It's all thanks to you that I can fly again."

"And thanks to you I now know what it's like to fly," said Lars, and he laughed happily, too.

Lars climbed to the top of the highest snow hill so that he could watch Yuri sailing home.

"Good-bye, Lars!" cried Yuri. "Next summer I will come to visit you. I promise!" Then he swooped down onto the departing ship.

After the ship disappeared over the horizon, the Little Polar Bear stayed at the top of his snow hill. This is high enough, he thought. I don't need to fly—I have a friend who can, and that's good enough for me!